Kevin Paul Johnson

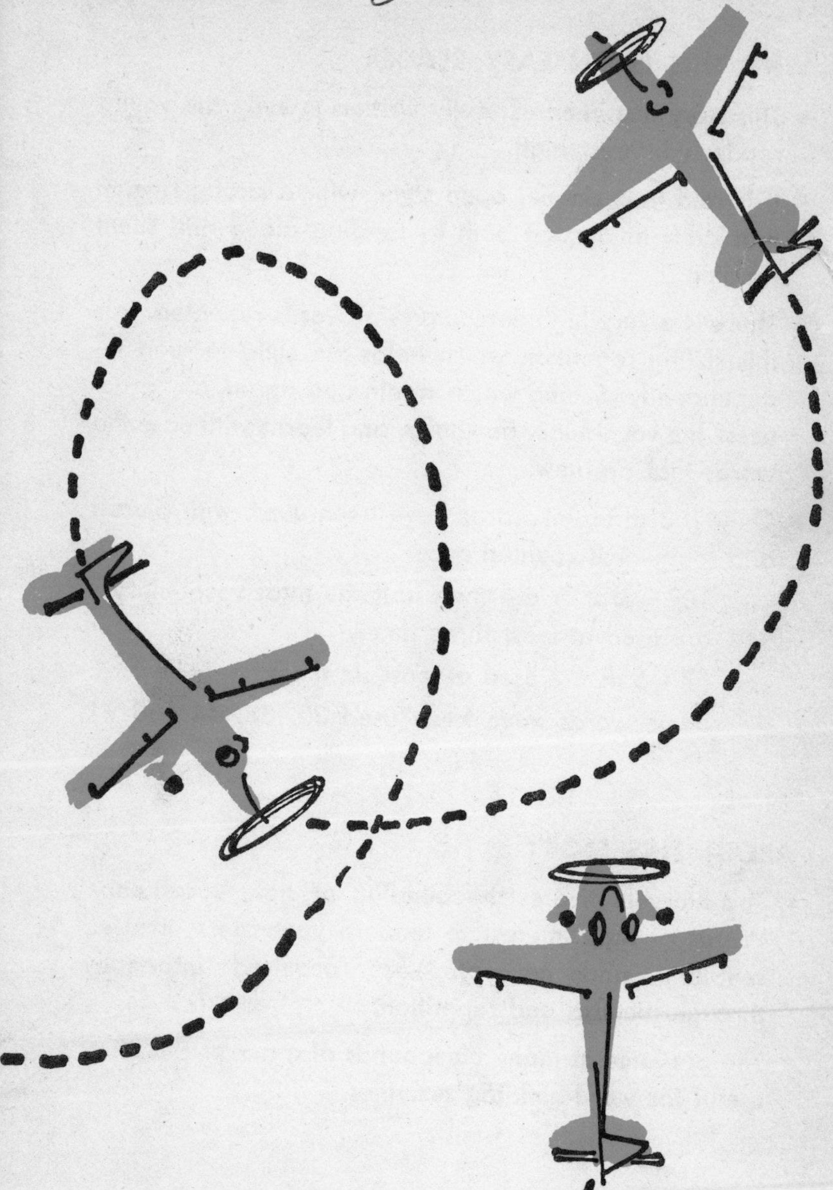

WHY THIS IS AN EASY READER

- This story has been carefully written to keep the young reader's interest high.

- It is told in a simple, open style, with a strong rhythm that adds enjoyment both to reading aloud and silent reading.

- There is a very high percentage of words repeated. It is this skillful repetition which helps the child to read independently. Seeing words again and again, he "practices" the vocabulary he knows, and learns with ease the words that are new.

- Only 183 different words have been used, with plurals and root words counted once.

    107 words—more than half the total vocabulary—are used at least three times.

    57 words are used at least six times.

    Some words have been used 30, 38, 44 and 71 times.

ABOUT THIS STORY

- This story motivates the building of sight vocabulary. Words of high interest to modern youngsters—like *jet, seaplane* and *helicopter*—are acquired informally through pictures and repetition.

- The presence of many compounds also makes this story useful for word-building activities.

FLY-AWAY
at the Air Show

Story by LEONE ADELSON
Pictures by ANDRÉE GOLBIN
Editorial Consultant: LILIAN MOORE

WONDER BOOKS · NEW YORK
A Division of Grosset & Dunlap, Inc.
A National General Company

Introduction

These books are meant to help the young reader discover what a delightful experience reading can be. The stories are such fun that they urge the child to try his new reading skills. They are so easy to read that they will encourage and strengthen him as a reader.

The adult will notice that the sentences aren't too long, the words aren't too hard, and the skillful repetition is like a helping hand. What the child will feel is: "This is a good story—and I can read it myself!"

For some children, the best way to meet these stories may be to hear them read aloud at first. Others, who are better prepared to read on their own, may need a little help in the beginning—help that is best given freely. Youngsters who have more experience in reading alone—whether in first or second or third grade—will have the immediate joy of reading "all by myself."

These books have been planned to help all young readers grow—in their pleasure in books and in their power to read them.

Lilian Moore
Specialist in Reading
Formerly of Division of Instructional Research,
New York City Board of Education

Fly-Away was a new little airplane
—as new as a new penny.
And he was bright, bright red.

7

Today Fly-Away was very happy.

For today was the big day

at Sky Top Airport.

8

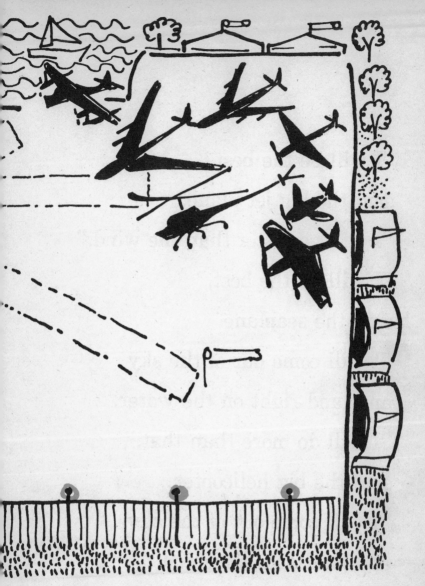

It was the day of the Air Show.
All the planes were going to do
tricks in the sky.

9

"I will be the best,"
said the big jet plane.
"I will go faster than the wind."
"I will be the best,"
said the seaplane.
"I will come out of the sky
and land right on the water."
"I will do more than that,"
said the big helicopter.
"I will come out of the sky
and land on a housetop."

"What about you, Little Fly-Away?"
asked Big Jet.

"Can you go faster than the wind?"

"No," said Fly-Away, "but—"

12

"Can you come out of the sky
and land on the water?"
asked Seaplane.

"No," said Fly-Away, "but—"

"Then can you come out of the sky
and land on a housetop?"
asked Big Helicopter.
"No, I cannot do that,"
said Fly-Away.

14

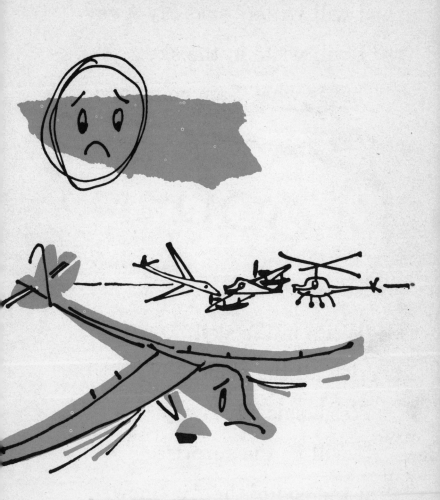

"What *are* you going to do
in the Air Show?"
they all wanted to know.

"I will write!" said Fly-Away.

"I will write in the sky.

That is what *I* am going to do

today!"

GOOD-BY.

"Write in the sky!"

cried all the planes.

"Yes," said Fly-Away.

"I will be the surprise

at the end of the Air Show. .

I will write

GOOD-BY. COME AGAIN.

I will surprise all the people."

16

There were so many people
to surprise!
There were boys and girls—
mothers and fathers—
grandmothers and grandfathers.

They were all waiting
for the Air Show to begin.

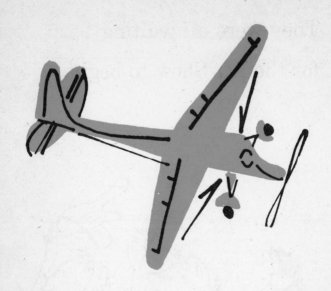

"Oh, wait till they see me

up there!"

said Fly-Away.

"Wait till they see

what I am going to do!"

Just then a gas truck came by,

and a man got out.

"Are you the plane that will write

in the sky?" he called.

"Yes," said Fly-Away.

"I am the one."

"Then here is the gas you need
to write with," the man said.

"Now you can make writing smoke."

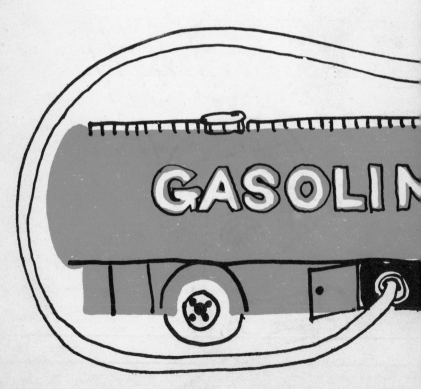

GASOLIN

It was time for the Air Show
to begin.

Zoo-oo-m!

Jet Plane was the first one
to take off.

He went so fast that soon no one
could see him.

"Hurray!" cried the people.

Br-r-r, br-r-r!

Then Seaplane took off.

Up, up, he went.

Then down he came,

right on the water—

and there he sat.

"Hurray!" cried the people.

Z-z-z-z! Big Helicopter took off next.

Up, up, he went.

Then he came down,

and there he was—

right on the housetop.

"Hurray!" cried the people.

"Wait till they see *me* up there,"

said Fly-Away.

"Wait till they see what *I* can do.

I wish I could go up right now!"

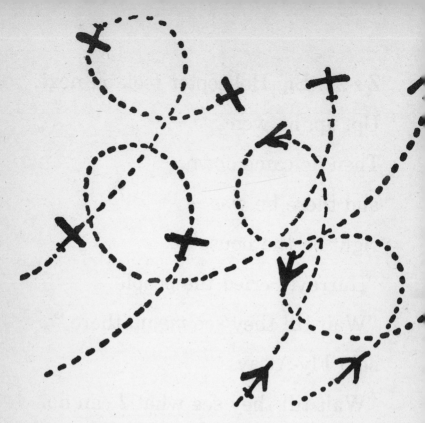

But Fly-Away had to wait.
There were more
airplane tricks to see.
There were planes
that did loop-the-loops.
There were planes
that flew upside down.

There were planes that took up some
jumpers.
Jump!
Jump!
Jump!

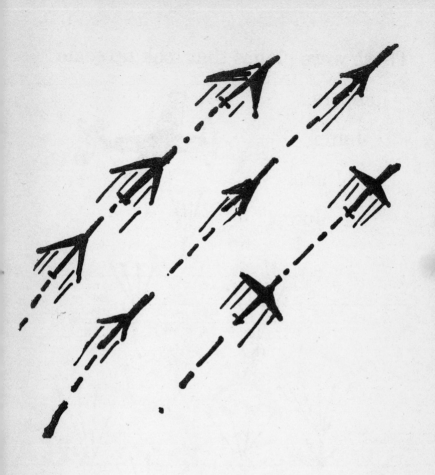

Out they came, one by one.

Down they came, one by one.

At last all the planes

came down, too.

It was time for Fly-away's surprise.

"Here I go!" cried Fly-Away.

P-p-pop! P-p-pop!

Fly-Away took off.

Up into the bright blue sky he went.

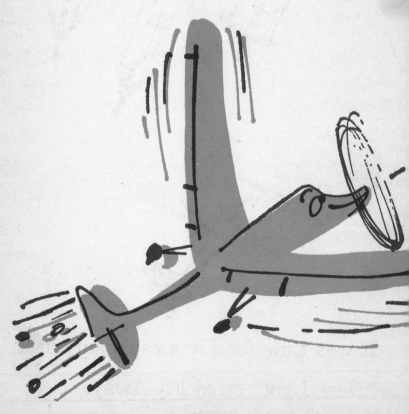

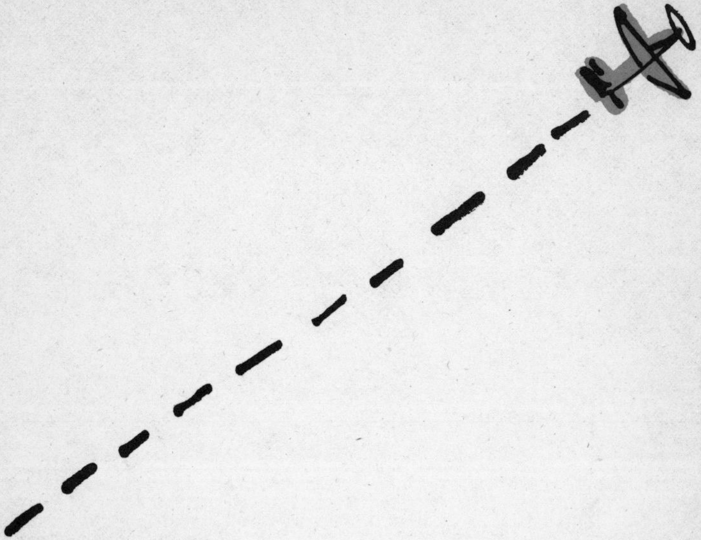

Fly-Away let out some smoke.

How white the smoke looked

in the blue sky!

"Good!" said Fly-Away.

"Now I will write

GOOD-BY. COME AGAIN."

Fly-Away let out some more smoke
and he flew on as fast as he could.
"There!" he said.
And he looked back.
But the smoke did not say
GOOD-BY.

"That's funny," said Fly-Away.

"Maybe I have to fly up."

Fly-Away let out some more
white smoke.

He flew way, way up.

Then he looked back.

The smoke did not say

GOOD-BY.

"That's *very* funny," said Fly-Away.

"Maybe I have to fly down."

So Fly-Away flew down.

Still the smoke did not say

GOOD-BY.

Fly-Away flew upside down.

He flew around and around.

But the white smoke

did not write

GOOD-BY. COME AGAIN.

It did not write anything.

"Oh, my!" said Fly-Away.

"The smoke is not making words."

"Maybe . . . maybe *I* have to make the words. But I don't know how! No one showed me how to write! Oh, what shall I do!"

Fly-Away looked down at the airport.

All the people were waiting

for the surprise.

Fly-Away had to do something.

But what could he do?

"I know!" cried Fly-Away.

"I can make pictures!

I can make smoke pictures!"

Fly-Away looked back at the sky.

Then he made a long line of smoke.

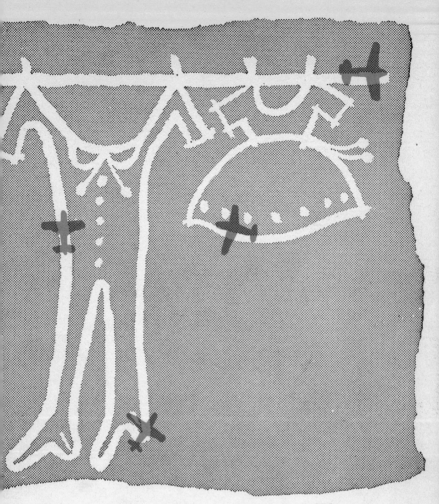

"Now," he said, "I will put
some things on that line."
And he did.
Then he flew off
to make a new picture.

"Hello," he called.

"What you need is this—

and this—

Good-by, Mr. Snowman."

and this—

and this—

Then Fly-Away did a loop-the-loop
in the sky.

"That looks like a hoop," he said.

"Let's see—a hoop needs a friend

to play with."

Fly-Away looked back at his picture.

"You need a friend, too," he said.

"There you are!" said Fly-Away.

"Now I will make a—"

But there was no more smoke!
Fly-Away could not make
any more pictures.
"Oh," said Fly-Away,
"I did not do
what I said I would do!
I did not write in the sky!
Everyone will laugh at me!"

But Fly-Away could not stay

up in the sky.

He had to go back to the airport.

Down went Fly-Away.

He did not want anyone to see him.

He wanted to hide.

But the planes saw him.

"Well!" said Big Helicopter.

"Well, well!" said Big Jet
and Seaplane.

"But no one showed me how
to write!" cried poor Fly-Away.

Just then the people began to shout.

"Sh! What's that?"

said Big Helicopter.

"Fly-Away! Fly-Away!"

the people shouted.

Fly-Away wanted to hide.

"Oh," he said,

"the people are mad at me."

The people shouted again.

"Hurray! Hurray for Fly-Away!"

"Hurray? Hurray for *me?*"
said the little red plane.
"But I did not know how to write!"
"Hurray for Fly-Away—the best
airplane in the Air Show!
Hurray for the smoke pictures!"
the people cried.

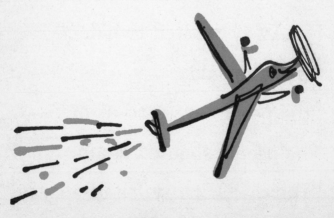

"The best airplane!

Was I the best airplane?"

said Fly-Away.

"Yes," said Big Jet. "Your pictures

were the best thing in the Air Show.

How do you like that, Fly-Away?"

"Oh, I like it," laughed Fly-Away.

"I like it very, very much!"

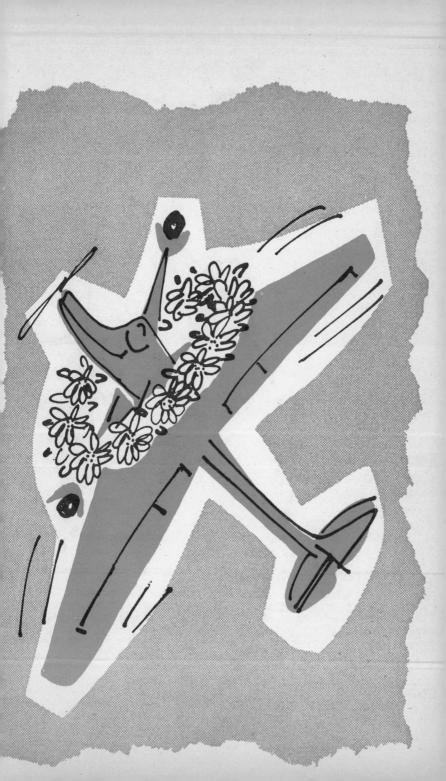

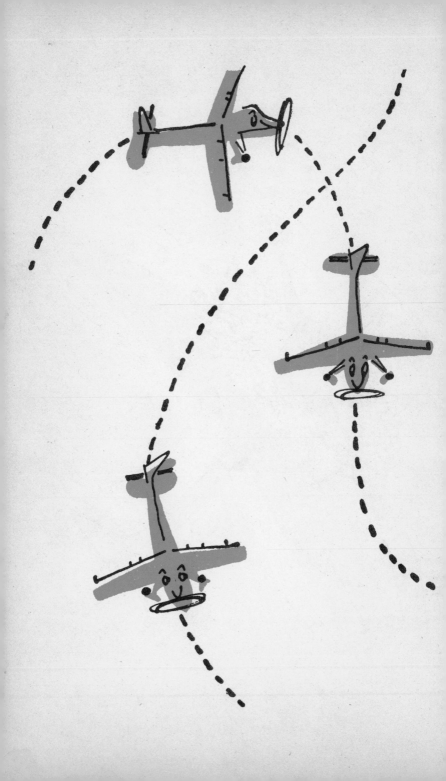